W9-BFZ-514

Officer Spence Makes No Sense!

Officer Spence Makes No Sense!

Beep!

Dan Gutman

Pictures by
Jim Paillot

HarperCollins*Publishers*

To Emma

Officer Spence Makes No Sense!

Text copyright © 2009 by Dan Gutman

Illustrations copyright © 2009 by Jim Paillot

Library of Congress Cataloging-in-Publication Data is available.

ISBN 978-0-06-155409-4 (pbk.) — ISBN 978-0-06-155410-0 (lib. bdg.)

Typography by Joel Tippie

09 10 11 12 13 LP/RRDB 10 9 8 7 6 5 4 3 2 1

❖

First Edition

Contents

The Mystery of the Missing PB&J

My name is A.J. and I hate school.

I was in the vomitorium eating lunch with the guys. Our lunch lady, Ms. LaGrange, was walking around saying hello to everybody.

"Bon appétit!" Ms. LaGrange said when she got to our table.

Ms. LaGrange is from France, so she's always saying weird stuff like "Bon appétit." I know that "appetite" means "being hungry" and "bon" means "bone." So when French people get hungry, I guess they eat bones.

French people are weird.

"I invented a new food!" Ms. LaGrange told us. "Would you like to try it?"

I never try new foods. That's the first rule of being a kid. New foods are yucky. We all looked in the bowl Ms. LaGrange was holding.

"What is it?" asked Ryan, who will eat anything, even stuff that isn't food.

"Take a guess," said Ms. LaGrange.

"Is it noodles?" asked Michael, who never ties his shoes.

"Not exactly," said Ms. LaGrange.

"Is it pasta?" asked Neil, who we call the nude kid even though he wears clothes.

"Nope," said Ms. LaGrange. "It's a combination of noodles *and* pasta."

"What's it called?" I asked.

"Poodlenasta!" said Ms. LaGrange.

Poodlenasta? Who names a food poodlenasta? Ms. LaGrange is strange.

Ryan tried some poodlenasta, but the rest of us said it looked gross. Neil opened his bag of Crispy Chips. Michael took out a bag of Crunchy Cheezy Crackos. My mom packed me a peanut butter and jelly sandwich.

I love peanut butter. And I love jelly. So peanut butter and jelly together is the perfect combination. The guy who invented the PB&J sandwich was a genius. He should get the No Bell Prize. That's a prize they give out to people who don't have bells.

This annoying girl named Andrea Young with curly brown hair was at the next table.* She was sitting with her crybaby friend Emily. Andrea thinks she

---

* I mean she was at the next table with her hair. If you were at one table and your hair was at another table, it would be weird.

is *so* smart because she's a member of P.A.C. That's the Principal Advisory Committee—a group of nerds who get to boss around the principal. Andrea was talking really loud to make sure we all heard her.

"Did you know that girls live longer than boys?" Andrea said.

"Really?" asked Emily. "I didn't know that."

"Yes, it's true," said Andrea. "I read it in my encyclopedia."

Andrea reads the encyclopedia for fun in her spare time. What is her problem? I slapped my head.

"Girls do *not* live longer than boys," I told her.

"Do too."

"Do not."

We went back and forth like that for a while.

"Boys would live longer if they ate healthy foods," said Andrea. "You shouldn't eat chips. They have a lot of fat in them."

"So does your face," I said.

"Oh, snap!" said Ryan.

I hate Andrea. Why can't a ton of chips fall on her head?

"So what are *you* eating?" Michael asked Andrea. "Nuts and berries and veggies?"

"My mom packed me some yummy tofu," Andrea told us.

"TOE FOOD?!" we all yelled.

I'd rather die young than eat food made from toes.

Andrea held up her fork with a piece of that toe food stuff on it. It was white. Ugh, disgusting! It looked like a big toe. I thought I was gonna throw up.

"Not 'toe food,' dumbheads!" Andrea said. "It's *tofu*!"

It sounded a lot like "toe food" to me.

That's when the most amazing thing in the history of the world happened. I opened my lunch box.

Well, that's not the amazing part, because I open my lunch box every day. The amazing part was that when I opened my lunch box, there was juice and a bag of chips in there, but *nothing else*!

My peanut butter and jelly sandwich was . . . *missing*!

Officer Spence Is Weird

My mom *never* forgets my peanut butter and jelly sandwich! I turned my lunch box upside down just to make sure the sandwich wasn't stuck to the bottom.

"Hey, which one of you stole my PB&J?" I asked the guys.

"Not me," said Ryan.

"Wasn't me," said Michael.

"Don't look at me," said Neil the nude kid.

That's when the weirdest thing in the history of the world happened. Our school security guard, Officer Spence, came running over really fast. He gets to carry cool stuff on his belt—a walkie-talkie, handcuffs, and one of those clubs they use to beat up bad guys on TV.

"Did I hear something about a stolen PB&J?" Officer Spence said. "That's the third one this week!"

"My mom probably forgot to pack it," I told him. "It's not a big deal."

"No, this looks like a robbery to me,"

said Officer Spence.

He grabbed his walkie-talkie and started shouting into it. "We have a Code Red at Ella Mentry School! A PB&J heist! Need backup! Fast! This is an emergency!"

"But Officer Spence, really, I don't need—"

I never had the chance to finish my sentence, because that's when five big guys in bulletproof vests came charging into the vomitorium! They surrounded our table. It was scary, but cool, too.

"Nobody move!" Officer Spence shouted at us. He took a roll of yellow tape out of his pocket and wrapped it around our chairs. "Don't touch anything! This is a

crime scene. Nobody leave this room. I'll have to question each of you."

Everybody in the vomitorium was shouting and screaming and freaking out.

That's when Mr. Klutz came over. He's the principal of Ella Mentry School, and he has no hair at all. I mean none. His head is so shiny, you can see yourself in it. Mr. Klutz was eating a sandwich.

"Is there the problem here?" he asked.

Suddenly, Officer Spence wheeled around and pointed his finger at Mr. Klutz as if it was a gun. It was just like policemen do to bad guys on TV.

"Freeze, dirtbag!" he yelled.

"WOW!" we all said, which is "MOM"
upside down.

On TV, the police always yell "Freeze,
dirtbag!" when they catch a bad guy
breaking the law. Nobody knows why.

But I never thought anybody would say "Freeze, dirtbag!" to the principal of a school. It was cool. Mr. Klutz put his hands in the air.

"Step away from the sandwich, Klutz, and nobody gets hurt!" Officer Spence said. "You're under arrest!"

"On what charge?" Mr. Klutz asked.

"Robbery!" said Officer Spence.

The Peanut Butter and Jelly Bandit

Officer Spence shoved Mr. Klutz against the wall and started searching through his pockets.

"You can't arrest the principal of our school!" said Andrea.

"Oh no?" Officer Spence said. "Just watch me."

"I didn't steal anything!" said Mr. Klutz.

"Oh no?" asked Officer Spence, holding up a spoon he found in Mr. Klutz's pocket. "What's *this*?"

"It's a spoon," Mr. Klutz said, "for my yogurt."

"Yogurt!" Officer Spence snorted. "Yeah, right! A spoon can be a deadly weapon, Klutz! You could gouge somebody's eyes out with one of those things. I'm going to have to confiscate this yogurt and do a DNA test on it."

"WHAT? Why?"

"You have the right to remain silent, Klutz," Officer Spence said. "So shut up!

Now open that briefcase. Nice and slow. And don't make any false moves!"

Mr. Klutz put his briefcase on the table and opened it.

"What have we *here*?" Officer Spence said as he held up two sandwiches.

"Those are peanut butter and jelly sandwiches," Mr. Klutz said.

"And I suppose you were going to eat a yogurt and *three* peanut butter and jelly sandwiches for lunch today, eh?" asked Officer Spence.

"That's right," Mr. Klutz said. "I *love* peanut butter and jelly."

"YOU'RE THE PEANUT BUTTER AND JELLY BANDIT!" Officer Spence yelled, pointing his finger at Mr. Klutz. "You steal food from hungry children. Is that the way you roll, Klutz?"

"No!" Mr. Klutz said. "My wife made those sandwiches for me. She makes my lunch every day."

Officer Spence grabbed the front of Mr. Klutz's shirt and yelled in his face. "That's right; blame it on your wife! You're pathetic, Klutz! I know how to handle punks like you."

"But—"

Officer Spence spun Mr. Klutz around and handcuffed his hands behind his back.

"But I didn't *do* anything!" Mr. Klutz

protested. "I'm the principal!"

"The criminal is always the one you least suspect," said Officer Spence.

At that moment, our vice principal, Mrs. Jafee, came rushing over.

"What's the doggone problem here?" she asked. "I heard some yelling."

"Freeze, dirtbag!" shouted Officer Spence. "You're under arrest!"

"WHAT!" yelled Mrs. Jafee as he handcuffed her.

"Take them away, boys!" Officer Spence shouted. "The two of 'em make me sick!"

The guys with bulletproof vests led Mr. Klutz and Mrs. Jafee out of the vomit-orium. We looked out the window and saw them get into a police car. The sirens were screaming and the lights were flashing as the police car drove away.

"WOW!" we all said again, which is "MOM" upside down.

I didn't like seeing Mr. Klutz and Mrs. Jafee get arrested, but I had to admit it was cool. A lot of weird things have happened at Ella Mentry

School, but this was the first time our principal and vice principal were taken away in handcuffs.

I looked at Ryan. Ryan looked at Michael. Michael looked at Neil. We were all looking at each other. Nobody knew what to say. Nobody except Andrea, of course.

"My name is Andrea, and I'm on the Principal's Advisory Committee," she said to Officer Spence. "Aren't you overreacting a little? I mean, it was just a sandwich."

"Just a sandwich, Andrea?" Officer Spence said, sneering. "Oh, you don't know the first thing about how the criminal mind works. First they steal a sandwich. If they get away with it, they come back the next day and take your whole lunch. And if you don't stop them right there, the next thing you know, they stole your refrigerator."

"You think Mr. Klutz is going to steal a refrigerator?" Michael asked.

"Believe me," Officer Spence said, "these dirtbags will steal anything that isn't nailed down."

"How would you nail down a refrigerator?" Ryan asked.

"With really long nails," I told him.

"Nobody leaves the school until I get to the bottom of this," Officer Spence announced.

"The bottom of what?" asked Neil the nude kid.

"I'm going to do a full-scale investigation," Officer Spence explained.

"You should try the nurse's office," I told him. "Mrs. Cooney has a scale in there that you can investigate."

Officer Spence stuck his face right next to mine.

"You think you're pretty funny, huh, punk?" he said. "Well, okay, Mr. Funny Boy. Just for that, *you* get to go *first*!"

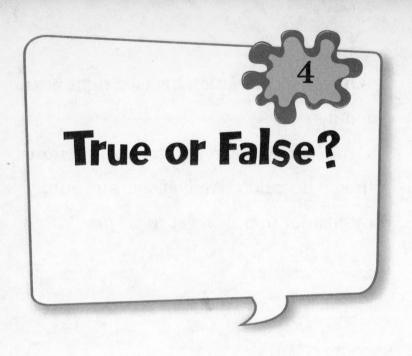

True or False?

Go first? Where? I didn't even know where I was going, but I sure didn't want to go there first.

Officer Spence took me to Room 104. That's Dr. Brad's room. He's our school counselor. He helps kids with their problems. But I don't have any problems,

so I don't have to
see him. Dr. Brad
doesn't come
to school
every day,
because
he works
at a bunch
of different
schools. So his
room was empty.

"Sit down!" ordered

Officer Spence.

I sat on the only chair in the room. There
were wires sticking out of it and leading
to a scary-looking machine on the table.

"Where's Mr. Klutz?" I asked. "What did you do with him?"

"He's probably in the slammer by now," Officer Spence replied.

Slammer? I never heard of a slammer. It sounded like some kind of a torture machine.

"What's a slammer?" I asked.

"He's in the pen," said Officer Spence.

"How could Mr. Klutz fit inside a pen?" I asked.

I didn't know what he was talking about. If Mr. Klutz was in a pen, it would have to be a really big pen. Where would the ink go? And how could anybody use a pen with a principal inside it?

"Mr. Klutz is in stir," said Officer Spence. "He's in the Big House. The cooler. The joint. The clink. The pokey. The hoosegow. The calaboose."

"Huh?"

"He's in JAIL!" Officer Spence shouted.

"Oh!" I said. "Why didn't you say so?"

"Never mind about Klutz," Officer Spence told me. "Ten peanut butter and jelly sandwiches have been stolen this month. There's a crime wave sweeping Ella Mentry School, and I'm going to put a stop to it once and for all."

Officer Spence looked really mad. He turned on the desk lamp and pointed it at my face. Then he hooked up a bunch of those scary wires to my arms and my head.

"What are you doing?" I asked.

"This machine is a lie detector," Officer Spence told me. "If you tell a lie, it will make a beeping sound. So you'd better tell the truth if you know what's good for you. Okay, let's get started. What's your name?"

"A.J."

I looked at the lie detector to see if it would beep. It didn't.

"Very good," said Officer Spence, "and what does A.J. stand for?"

"Arlo Jervis," I admitted.

"That's right," Officer Spence said. "The lie detector didn't beep. So you must be telling the truth. Good boy. Do you like school, A.J.?"

"No," I said.

"That's true also," he said. "Tell me, Arlo Jervis, is there *anything* you like about school?"

"No," I said.

BEEP!

"That's a lie!" Officer Spence said. "You like something. Or somebody."

"I do not," I said.

BEEP!

"Liar!" shouted Officer Spence. "I bet you like Andrea, that girl in your class with the curly brown hair, right?"

"I do not!" I said.

BEEP!

"You're lying!"

"I am not!" I shouted. "I hate Andrea!"

BEEP!

"Liar!" shouted Officer Spence. "You're secretly in love with Andrea, aren't you?"

"No!"

BEEP!

"Hey!" I said. "What does any of this have to do with the stolen peanut butter and jelly sandwich?"

"Oh, yeah, the sandwich," said Officer Spence. "Did you steal it?"

"No!" I said. "How could I steal it? It was *my* sandwich! And I didn't even get to eat it!"

Officer Spence was going to ask me another question, but you'll never believe who walked into the door at that moment.

Nobody, because if you walked into a door it would hurt. But you'll never believe who opened the door and walked into the room.

It was Andrea! And right behind her were Emily, Ryan, and Michael.

"I'm on the Principal's Advisory Committee," said Andrea. "It says right here in the *Ella Mentry School Handbook* that you can't give lie detector tests to students without their parents' permission."

"Let me see that!" Officer Spence demanded.

Andrea handed him the *Ella Mentry School Handbook* and showed him a page in it.

"See?" she said.

"Fine!" Officer Spence replied. "I'll find another way to nab the peanut butter and jelly sandwich bandit. I've seen these criminals in action. They'll take anything that's not nailed down."

"So we should nail down our sandwiches?" asked Michael.

"If you nailed down a sandwich, it would be hard to eat," said Ryan.

"You could eat around the nail," I pointed out.

"Quiet!" barked Officer Spence. "You

kids think you're pretty smart, don't you? Do you think peanut butter and jelly sandwiches grow on trees?"

"No," we all said.

I tried to imagine a peanut butter and jelly sandwich growing on a tree. That would be cool. When you were hungry, you could just go outside and pick a sandwich.

"I hope they throw the book at you kids," Officer Spence muttered.

"Why would they throw a book at us?" asked Michael.

"Throwing a book might ruin the binding," said Emily. "Mrs. Roopy, the librarian, says you shouldn't throw books.

You should treat them with TLC. That stands for 'tender loving care.'"

"Enough!" yelled Officer Spence. "When I'm through with you kids, they might give you the chair."

"Why would they give us a chair?" I asked.

"So if you steal a sandwich they give you a chair?" asked Ryan. "That's weird."

"What if you have all the chairs you need?" asked Michael.

"I said that's ENOUGH!" yelled Officer Spence. "Oh, by the way, Andrea, Arlo Jervis here is in love with you."

"Ooooooooooooooo," everybody said.

"Is that true, Arlo?" asked Andrea, all smiley. "I always thought you secretly liked me."

"I don't!" I shouted.

BEEP!

"It *is* true!" Andrea said.

"It is not!" I yelled.

BEEP!

"Oooooh!" Ryan said. "A.J. and Andrea are in *love*!"

"When are you gonna get married?" asked Michael.

"Never!" I yelled.

BEEP!

If those guys weren't my best friends, I would hate them.

"You kids are no help at all," Officer Spence shouted. "Get out of here! Go back to class. I'll find the peanut butter and jelly bandit by myself."

I'll tell you, Officer Spence makes no sense.

Nah-Nah-Nah Boo-Boo

5

Y'know how your teacher says you have to read a chapter in a book before you can have fun? And you really don't want to? Well, read *this* chapter. Then go have fun! And tell your teacher nah-nah-nah boo-boo!

Searching for Clues

When I got back to class, Mrs. Patty, our school secretary, made an announcement over the loudspeaker.

"Attention, all teachers and students," Mrs. Patty said. "This will be a perfectly normal day at Ella Mentry School. Continue with your lessons as scheduled.

Principal Spence is now in charge."

"PRINCIPAL SPENCE?!" we all said.

"He's taking over the school," whispered Ryan, who was sitting next to me. "He's crazy!"

Our teacher, Mr. Granite, had been talking about protecting the environment, as usual. Mr. Granite is an alien. No, really, I mean it! Mr. Granite is from another planet. It's called Etinarg, which is "granite" spelled backward.

"Here's a little trick to save water," said Mr. Granite. "Put an empty bucket on the floor of your shower. While you wait for the water to warm up, the bucket will catch some of the cold water. Then you can use it to water your plants."

Mr. Granite is always giving us tips to save energy. But that's when something weird happened. A head appeared in the doorway. It was Officer Spence's head. He was crawling around on the ground, and he was looking through a magnifying glass.

"Uh, what are you doing, Officer Spence?" asked Mr. Granite.

"Searching for clues," Officer Spence replied. "I'm trying to nab the peanut butter and jelly bandit."

"But you already said the peanut butter and jelly bandit was Mr. Klutz," said Michael.

"Klutz is just one suspect," Officer

Spence said. "This could be a conspiracy."

I never heard *that* word before.

"A conspiracy?" I asked. "What's that?"

"A conspiracy is a secret agreement between two or more people to break the law," said Andrea, all proud of herself.

"Could you possibly be more boring?" I asked Andrea.

Little Miss I-Know-Everything keeps a dictionary on her desk to look up words. That way she can show everybody how smart she is.

"Aha!" Officer Spence suddenly shouted. "I found a clue!"

"What is it?" Emily asked. "What did you find?"

"A hair," said Officer Spence.

"So?" we all asked.

"This is proof that the peanut butter and jelly bandit has hair," Officer Spence announced.

"Well, Mr. Klutz doesn't have any hair at all," Mr. Granite told him. "So he must be innocent, right?"

"Yes, but *you've* got hair, don't you?" Officer Spence said, looking at Mr. Granite.

"Well, yes, but I didn't steal—"

Mr. Granite didn't have the chance to finish his sentence, because at that moment Officer Spence jumped up and pointed his finger at him like it was a gun.

"Freeze, dirtbag! You're under arrest!"

"That's not even a gun," said Mr. Granite.

"Maybe I have a gun hidden inside my finger," said Officer Spence. "Hands up!"

"What did I do?" Mr. Granite said, putting his hands up. "I don't even *have* a peanut butter and jelly sandwich."

"No, but you're an illegal alien!" shouted Officer Spence.

"Well, that's true," admitted Mr. Granite as Officer Spence put handcuffs on him. "I am from the planet Etinarg."

"Are you going to send Mr. Granite to jail too?" asked Neil the nude kid.

"No," said Officer Spence.

"Whew, that's a relief!" said Andrea.

"I don't need to send him to jail," Officer Spence told us. "I brought the jail *here*."

WHAT?!

He went out in the hallway and came back in wheeling a big cage. It was sort of like a portable jail.

"WOW," we all said, which is "MOM" upside down.

"Where did you get *that*?" I asked.

"Rent-A-Jail," said Officer Spence as he pushed Mr. Granite into the cell. "You can rent anything."

"This is not fair! You can't do this!" Mr. Granite protested. "I have my rights!"

"Yeah, you have the right to remain

silent," said Officer Spence. "So shut up!"

"Help! Help!" shouted Mr. Granite as the jail cell was wheeled away. "Let me *ouuuuuuuuuuuttttttt*!"

You Can't Say "Butt" in a Children's Book

Well, it was sure shaping up to be an exciting day at Ella Mentry School! First our principal and vice principal were sent to jail. Then our teacher was arrested.

We didn't have much time to think about it, because we had to go to reading class with our reading specialist, Mr. Macky. I hate to read, but sometimes it's fun, because Mr. Macky is wacky.

"Open your books to page thirty-four," Mr. Macky said. "Today we're going to read a story called *The Happy Bunny*. Don't you just love bunnies?"

"Yes!" yelled all the girls.

"No!" yelled all the boys.

"'Bixby the Bunny was a happy little bunny,'" Mr. Macky read from the book. "'He loved to eat carrots and chase butterflies and frolic in the morning sun. But then one day—'"

Mr. Macky didn't have the chance to finish his sentence, because the strangest thing in the history of the world happened. Officer Spence burst into the room.

"Freeze, dirtbag!" he yelled. "Step away from that book and nobody gets hurt, Macky!"

"Gasp!" everybody gasped.

"What's the problem?" asked Mr. Macky. "I was just reading *The Happy Bunny* to the kids. What did I do wrong?"

"Don't act all innocent!" shouted Officer Spence. "That story has the word 'but' in it!"

"So?" Emily said.

"What's wrong with the word 'but'?" asked Mr. Macky.

"Don't play cute with me, mister!" shouted Officer Spence. "I know what you meant."

"What did he mean?" asked Michael.

"B-U-T-T!" spelled out Officer Spence. "And you can't use the word *B-U-T-T* in a children's book!"

"I didn't say *B-U-T-T!*" explained Mr. Macky. "I said *B-U-T!*"

"Sounds like *B-U-T-T* to me," said Officer Spence.

"Sort of like 'toe food' and 'tofu,'" I pointed out.

"Quiet, Arlo!" said Andrea. "This is serious!"

She was right, because Officer Spence went out in the hall and came back in wheeling another one of those portable jail cells.

"Wait a minute!" Mr. Macky said. "What's wrong with the word 'butt' anyway? It's just a body part."

Officer Spence stopped and glared at Mr. Macky from way too close to his face.

"Just a body part?" he said. "It's the body part you sit on! So that makes it bad. We can't have potty mouths like you teaching young children! If kids think it's okay to say *B-U-T-T*, they might start saying other body parts, like *E-L-B-O-W* or *E-A-R-L-O-B-E*. And we can't have that."

"Look for yourself!" Mr. Macky said, holding up *The Happy Bunny*. "It doesn't even say *B-U-T-T*. It says *B-U-T*."

"It was a typo," Officer Spence said. "They meant to write *B-U-T-T*. They forgot the second *T*."

"This is ridiculous!" said Mr. Macky. "I'm sure *lots* of books have that word in them."

"Lots of people rob banks!" Officer Spence said. "You think that makes it right? Get in the cell, Macky!"

"But—"

"You said it AGAIN!" Officer Spence yelled as he pushed Mr. Macky into the jail cell. "And you call yourself a reading specialist? How do you sleep at night? You disgust me!"

"I didn't DO anything!" Mr. Macky shouted. "I'm an innocent man!"

"You have the right to remain silent," said Officer Spence. "So shut up!"

"No! Let me *ouuuuuuuuuuuttttttttttt*!"

Mrs. Cooney Is Busted

What a weird day it was! Officer Spence was arresting grown-ups left and right!

After reading, we had to go to the nurse's room for health. Our school nurse is Mrs. Cooney. She has eyes that look like cotton candy, and she is beautiful. She wanted to marry me a while back, but

I told her I wouldn't marry her because she's already married to some guy named Mr. Cooney.

Mrs. Cooney was teaching us about Hi Jean.*

"You should wash your hands every time you use the bathroom," she told us. "That will prevent the spread of germs that make us—"

She didn't have the chance to finish her sentence, because that's when Officer Spence burst into the room.

"Freeze, dirtbag!" he yelled.

"What's the meaning of this?" asked

---

* That's what you say when you meet somebody named Jean.

Mrs. Cooney, putting her hands up. "I
didn't do anything."

"I want you to open that cabinet over
the sink slowly," Officer Spence ordered.

"And then back away. No false moves, Cooney!"

Mrs. Cooney went and opened the cabinet over the sink. There were some bandages in there and some bottles of aspirin.

"Aha!" Officer Spence hollered. "Aspirin! Can you get that stuff in a drugstore?"

"Well, yes, of course," Mrs. Cooney said.

"Just as I suspected!" Officer Spence shouted. "You're a drug dealer!"

"WHAT?!"

"You're handing out drugs to innocent children!" Officer Spence yelled as he wheeled in a portable jail cell. "You should be ashamed of yourself. How do you sleep at night?"

"I take NyQuil," Mrs. Cooney said.

"Get in the cell, Cooney, and nobody gets hurt!"

"But I didn't—"

"You have the right to remain silent," yelled Officer Spence. "So shut up!"

"No! Help! Let me *goooooooooooooooooo*!"

"Are you going to do a full-scale investigation?" I asked. "There's the scale."

"Quiet, you!" said Officer Spence.

He told us to be on our best behavior while he wheeled Mrs. Cooney's jail cell over to where the other arrested grown-ups were. So as soon as he left the room, me and Michael and Ryan got up and shook our butts at the class. Most of the kids laughed. Except for Little Miss I-Never-Do-Anything-Wrong.

"You know, you shouldn't be joking around, Arlo," Andrea said. "This whole thing is your fault."

"My fault?" I said. "What did I do?"

"If you had checked your lunch box before coming to school, you would have noticed that your sandwich was missing," said Andrea. "Then none of this would have happened."

I hate Andrea.

We were all sitting there in the nurse's

office without any grown-ups. I looked at Michael. Michael looked at Ryan. Ryan looked at Andrea. Andrea looked at Emily. Emily looked at Neil the nude kid. We were all looking at each other.

"Maybe Officer Spence isn't a real security guard," I said. "Did you ever think of that?"

"Yeah," Michael said, "maybe he kidnapped our real security guard and has him locked up in a cage. Just like he's locking up all the teachers. Stuff like that happens all the time, you know."

"Stop trying to scare Emily," said Andrea.

Emily looked like she was going to cry. As usual.

"Officer Spence is crazy!" Ryan said. "There's no telling what he'll do next."

"He might put us *all* in jail!" said Neil the nude kid.

"We've got to *do* something!" Emily said, and then she went running out of the room.

Well, at least we got rid of her. She is such a crybaby.

"Emily was right," said Neil. "We've got to do something."

"What can we do, call the police?" asked Andrea. "Officer Spence *is* the police."

Andrea was right, for once in her life.

There was nothing we could do.

That's when I got the greatest idea in the history of the world. On the wall in the nurse's office is a little red box that says FIRE: IN CASE OF EMERGENCY, BREAK GLASS.

"Are you thinking what I'm thinking?" I said to the guys.

"Yeah!" said the guys.

"Is this an emergency?" I asked.

"Definitely," said the guys.

"Arlo, don't!" Andrea yelled.

She tried to stop me, but I was too fast for her. I pulled the fire alarm.*

---

* Don't do this at school as a joke. EVER.

Officer Spence Is Getting Weirder

BRING!BRING!BRING!BRING!

Fire alarm bells always go *BRING!BRING!BRING!BRING!* Nobody knows why.

It was really loud! We had to hold our hands over our ears. Everybody was freaking out. It was cool.

"Get outside!" people were screaming in the hallways. "Fire! Everybody outside!"

When we got out to the playground, it was like a war zone. Officer Spence had put barbed wire on top of the fence. There was a helicopter hovering over the school. Officer Spence was wearing a camouflage suit, and he was running around with a weird helmet over his face.

"What's that he's wearing?" Ryan asked.

"Night vision goggles," Michael told us. "They let you see in the dark. I saw them in a movie once."

"Night vision goggles are cool," I said.

"But why is he wearing night vision goggles in the middle of the day?" asked Neil.

"Because he's crazy!" Andrea said.

Officer Spence was running around, arresting every grown-up he could find. First he ran over to our science teacher, Mr. Docker.

"Freeze, dirtbag!" he yelled.

"What did I do?" asked Mr. Docker.

"You're conducting bizarre experiments in the science lab," Officer Spence said. "You're under arrest."

He put handcuffs on Mr. Docker. Then he ran over to our bus driver, Mrs. Kormel.

"Freeze, dirtbag!"

"What did I do?" she asked.

"I saw you drinking and driving," accused Officer Spence.

"It was coffee!" said Mrs. Kormel.

"Yes, and you were *drinking* it," Officer Spence said as he handcuffed her. "Drinking and driving is against the law, so you're under arrest!"

Then he ran over to our crossing guard, Mr. Louie. He was holding his guitar that looks like a stop sign.

"Freeze, dirtbag!"

"Hey man, like, y'know?" said Mr. Louie, making a peace sign. "Can't we all learn to love one another and live in peace and harmony?"

"No!" Officer Spence barked. "You're under arrest!"

"Hey, I'm just chillin', dude," Mr. Louie said. "Doin' my thing. Like, can you dig it? Why are you hassling me, bro?"

"Because you stand out in the middle of the street before and after school," Officer Spence said.

"Yeah, that's my job, man," Mr. Louie said. "Like, I'm a crossing guard? I gotta help the kids cross the street. It's what I do. Can you dig where I'm comin' from?"

"You're a jaywalker!" Officer Spence yelled. "And you're going to jail!"

"Oh, man!" Mr. Louie said as he was handcuffed. "Lighten up, dude! Like, y'know? You're giving off bad vibes and bumming everybody out."

"You have the right to remain silent," said Officer Spence. "So shut up!"

"No! Like, help! Let me *goooooooooooo*!"

10

The Peanut Butter and Jelly Bandit Is . . .

Officer Spence ordered us kids to go back inside the school and wait for him in the all-purpose room. That's a room we use for all purposes, so it has the perfect name. I looked at the clock as we went into school. It was almost three o'clock. Soon it would be time to go home.

We got to the all-purpose room, and it was amazing! The whole stage was filled with a long line of jail cells. Each one had a different grown-up in it—Mrs. Roopy, Mrs. Yonkers, Ms. Hannah, Mr. Loring, Miss Small. They were all there.

"WOW!" we said, which is "MOM" upside down.

"Help! Help! Let us out!" The teachers were yelling and rattling their cages. "Officer Spence is crazy!"

"You have the right to remain silent!" Officer Spence yelled at them. "So shut up!"

I had to admit, the whole thing was pretty cool. It was a lot like going to the

zoo, except there were teachers in the cages instead of monkeys, bears, and baboons.

It was a real Kodak moment. You should have been there!

"There aren't any more grown-ups for Officer Spence to arrest," Ryan whispered.

"What's he gonna do now?"

"Beats me," I said.

Officer Spence climbed up on the stage and grabbed the microphone.

"Okay, I have looked over all the evidence," he announced. "I examined fingerprints. I looked at hair samples under a microscope. I got the results of the DNA tests. And now I know the truth. I know who the guilty party is. The peanut butter and jelly bandit is . . ."

I leaned forward in my seat. We *all* leaned forward in our seats. It was really suspenseful! Everybody got quiet. You could hear a pin drop. But not one of those little pins you use for sewing clothes. Those pins don't make any noise when you drop them. I tried that once, and I couldn't hear it at all. I mean like a bowling pin. Because they make a lot of noise when they drop.

Bowling is fun. I got a 109 once. I'm going bowling on Saturday because I got invited to Neil the nude kid's birthday party. They're going to put up bumpers so we can't throw any gutter balls.

But that doesn't have anything to do with all the suspense that was in the all-purpose room.

"The peanut butter and jelly bandit is . . ."

Officer Spence didn't have the chance to finish his sentence. Because at that moment, the most amazing thing in the history of the world happened.

But I'm not going to tell you what it was.

Okay, okay, I'll tell you. But you have to read the next chapter to find out. So nah-nah-nah boo-boo on you!

Skippy and Jif Save the Day

Officer Spence was about to name the peanut butter and jelly bandit when we heard this loud grinding noise. It sounded like it was coming from under the stage.

Then there was a banging noise. *BANG! BANG! BANG!*

And then, right next to Officer Spence,

this *thing* popped up from under the stage! It was tan-colored, and it looked like a balloon or a beach ball or something.

"A tan-colored beach ball is coming through the floor!" I hollered.

"No, I think it's a giant sea serpent!" yelled Ryan.

"It looks like an enormous lightbulb!" shouted Michael.

"Run for your lives!" screamed Neil the nude kid.

But then we all realized that the thing that was coming up through the floor wasn't a balloon or a beach ball or a giant sea serpent or an enormous lightbulb. You'll never believe in a million hundred years what it was.

It was Mr. Klutz's shiny bald head!

Our principal, Mr. Klutz, climbed out from under the stage. He was wearing a prison uniform.

"Hooray for Mr. Klutz!" all the teachers shouted.

Coming up right behind Mr. Klutz was our vice principal, Mrs. Jafee! She was wearing a prison uniform, too, and she had two dogs with her.

"We thought you were in jail!" shouted Michael.

"We *were* in jail, you betcha," Mrs. Jafee said. "We tunneled out using our yogurt spoons."

"I'm starved," said Mr. Klutz. "Does anybody have any yogurt?"

Officer Spence looked really mad. He wheeled around and pointed his finger at Mr. Klutz and Mrs. Jafee like it was a gun.

"Freeze, dirtbags!" he yelled. "You're under arrest . . . again! In fact, you're *all* under arrest!"

"*All* of us?" asked Andrea.

"That's right," Officer Spence said. "Kids

too. The whole school. Everybody's under arrest! You're all going to jail. Hands up!"

Four hundred kids put our hands in the air. Mrs. Jafee's dogs started nosing around the stage like they were trying to smell something.

"What cute dogs!" said Andrea, who never misses the chance to brownnose a grown-up. "What are their names?"

"Skippy and Jif," said Mrs. Jafee. "They're peanut butter–sniffing dogs."

Peanut butter–sniffing dogs? I heard of dogs that sniff out bombs. I heard of dogs that sniff out drugs. But I never heard of dogs that sniff out peanut butter! Maybe Mrs. Jafee was yanking our chain.

"Where did you get peanut butter–sniffing dogs?" asked Emily.

"From Rent-A-Peanut-Butter–Sniffing-Dog," said Mr. Klutz. "You can rent anything."

"Ruff!" barked Skippy.

"Get those dogs out of here!" shouted Officer Spence. "You can't have dogs in school!"

The dogs were sniffing all around Officer Spence.

"Ruff!" barked Jif.

"You dogs are under arrest," Officer Spence yelled. "Put your paws up! You have the right to remain silent—"

But Officer Spence didn't have the chance to finish his sentence because suddenly, Skippy pulled something out of Officer Spence's pocket.

It was a sandwich!

A peanut butter and jelly sandwich!

"GASP!" everybody gasped.

"Oh, snap!" said Ryan.

"How did that get in my pocket?" asked Officer Spence. "Who put it there?"

"I'll tell you who put it there," Mr. Klutz said. "*You* put it there! Because *you*, Officer

Spence, are the *real* peanut butter and jelly bandit!"

"GASP!" everybody gasped again.

"I didn't see *that* coming!" Ryan said to me.

"You said it yourself," Mr. Klutz told Officer Spence. "The criminal is always

the one you least suspect!"

The teachers started rattling their cages and shouting. Now that everybody knew Officer Spence was the peanut butter and jelly bandit, we all started booing him.

"BOOOOOOOOOOOOOOOOOO!"

"Throw the book at him!" yelled Michael.

"Put him in the pen!" yelled Ryan.

"Give him the chair!" yelled Neil the nude kid.

But Mr. Klutz held up his hand and made a peace sign. When a grown-up makes a peace sign at our school, it means we have to shut up. Nobody knows why.

"Why did you do it, Officer Spence?"

Mr. Klutz asked. "Why did you turn to a life of crime?"

"I . . . I . . ."

Officer Spence didn't have the chance to finish his sentence. Because you'll never believe in a million hundred years who came into the all-purpose room at that moment.

It was Dr. Brad, the school counselor!

The Truth About Officer Spence

Dr. Brad climbed up on the stage. He's an old guy with frizzy hair and a cane. He talks funny.*

"I know vye he deed eet," Dr. Brad said.

"Vye?" asked Mr. Klutz. "I mean, why?

---

* Ask your mom or dad or teacher to read Dr. Brad's part. It will be hilarious.

Why did he do it?"

Dr. Brad put his arm around Officer Spence's shoulder. Officer Spence looked all sad.

"Ven you ver a leetle boy, you vatched thee brave policemen on thee television and in zee movies, yes?"

"Yes," said Officer Spence.

"They ver heroes to you, yes?"

"Yes."

"And you vanted to grow up and become like von of zem, fighting crime, yes?"

"Yes."

"But zee boys und girls at our school are so nice, zer eez no crime to fight here, yes? So you decided to invent some crime, yes? And zen you vould be zee beeg hero, yes?"

"Yes," said Officer Spence. He was whimpering now, like a kid who lost his dog or something.

"Tell me about your childhood," Dr. Brad said. "It vasn't happy, no?"

"No."

"Somezing bad happened to you ven you ver a leetle boy, yes?"

"Yes."

"Eet vas somezing with peanut butter, yes?"

"Yes!"

"Mommy vouldn't geeve you peanut butter, vould she?"

"It's true! It's all true!" Officer Spence whimpered. He was totally crying now. "Mommy wouldn't let me have peanut butter. All the other kids had peanut butter every day. But my mommy wouldn't give it to me. Ever! Why? Why? Why?"

Wow, Dr. Brad should be in the gifted and talented program! He had Officer Spence sobbing and blubbering all over the stage. And we got to see it live and in person.

Mr. Klutz handed Officer Spence a tissue, and he blew his nose into it. Well, I mean, he just blew his nose. If you blew your nose into a tissue, your nose would fall off. You'd have a tissue with a nose in it. And a hole in your face. That would be weird.

"And how did you feel ven Mommy vouldn't geeve you zee peanut butter?" Dr. Brad asked.

"Angry," Officer Spence said. "Hurt. I had to eat jelly sandwiches with no peanut butter. I *hate* jelly sandwiches! All I wanted was a little peanut butter on my sandwich.

Was that too much to ask? But Mommy wouldn't give it to me! Boo hoo!"

"And zat eez vye you took zee sandwiches, yes?"

"Yes. I'm sorry," Officer Spence said. "I didn't mean to. I won't do it anymore. And I'll stop carving peanut butter sculptures in my basement, too."

"You carve peanut butter sculptures in your basement?" asked Mr. Klutz.

Yuck. Disgusting! I thought I was gonna throw up.

Officer Spence wiped his eyes and blew his nose again. Sheesh, get a grip! That guy is a bigger crybaby than Emily.

"There, there," Mr. Klutz said as he gave

Officer Spence a hug. "Everything is going to be all right."

"Zees man does not need to go to jail," said Dr. Brad. "He needs help."

"We'll get him the help he needs," said Mr. Klutz.

Dr. Brad and Mr. Klutz put their arms around Officer Spence, and together they walked away into the sunset.

Well, they didn't really walk away into the sunset. In the movies, people always walk away into the sunset at the end. That would have been cool, except that it was three o'clock in the afternoon. And even though we call it the all-purpose room, watching the sunset isn't one of the purposes. If you're going to have a happy ending, you should always schedule it around sunset in a place where you can actually walk into it.

It didn't matter, because that's when the bell rang. It was time to go home! We all rushed out the door, screaming our heads off. My mom was waiting in the car for me, because I had to go to the dentist after school.

"How was school?" my mom asked as I got in the car.

"Fine."

"Did anything exciting happen today, A.J.?"

I thought about how Officer Spence

went crazy and arrested all the grown-ups. I thought about how he put them in cages. I thought about how Mr. Klutz and Mrs. Jafee broke out of jail and tunneled their way back to school with yogurt spoons. I thought about how Dr. Brad made Officer Spence start crying.

"Nah," I told my mom. "Nothing exciting happened. It was a really boring day."

Well, I wasn't gonna tell *her* what happened! She would just think I made it all up.

"That's nice," Mom said as she pulled away from the curb. "Oh, by the way, I forgot to pack your peanut butter and jelly sandwich this morning. Here, you

can eat it now."

Man, that was the best peanut butter and jelly sandwich I ever tasted!

Well, that's pretty much what happened. Maybe Officer Spence will stop arresting people and stealing their sandwiches. Maybe we'll get a new security guard who doesn't have peanut butter problems. Maybe Ms. LaGrange will start a company that sells poodlenasta. Maybe Andrea will get kicked off the Principal's Advisory Committee. Maybe Mrs. Jafee will get her own book. Maybe a truck full of peanut butter and jelly sandwiches will fall on Andrea's head. Maybe Dr. Brad will stop talking funny. Maybe Mr. Klutz will finally get to eat his yogurt. Maybe Rent-A-Jail will give Officer Spence his money back. Maybe a museum will put his peanut butter sculptures on display. Maybe we'll figure out why so much weird stuff is always happening at our school.

But it won't be easy!

Check out the My Weird School series!

#1: Miss Daisy Is Crazy!

The first book in the hilarious series stars A.J., a second grader who hates school—and can't believe his teacher hates it too!

#2: Mr. Klutz Is Nuts!

A.J. can't believe his crazy principal wants to climb to the top of the flagpole!

#3: Mrs. Roopy Is Loopy!

The new librarian thinks she's George Washington one day and Little Bo Peep the next!

#4: Ms. Hannah Is Bananas!

The art teacher wears clothes made from pot holders. Worse than that, she's trying to make A.J. be partners with yucky Andrea!

#5: Miss Small Is off the Wall!

The gym teacher is teaching A.J.'s class to juggle scarves, balance feathers, and do everything *but* play sports!

#6: Mr. Hynde Is Out of His Mind!

The music teacher plays bongo drums on the principal's bald head! But does he have what it takes to be a real rock-and-roll star?

#7: Mrs. Cooney Is Loony!

The school nurse is everybody's favorite—but is she hiding a secret identity?

#8: Ms. LaGrange Is Strange!

The new lunch lady talks funny—and why is she writing secret messages in the mashed potatoes?

#9: Miss Lazar Is Bizarre!

What kind of grown-up *likes* cleaning throw-up? Miss Lazar is the weirdest custodian in the world!

#10: Mr. Docker Is off His Rocker!

The science teacher alarms and amuses A.J.'s class with his wacky experiments and nutty inventions.

#11: Mrs. Kormel Is Not Normal!
A.J.'s school bus gets a flat tire, then becomes hopelessly lost at the hands of the wacky bus driver.

#12: Ms. Todd Is Odd!
Ms. Todd is subbing, and A.J. and his friends are sure she kidnapped Miss Daisy so she could take over her job.

#13: Mrs. Patty Is Batty!
A little bit of spookiness and a lot of humor add up to the best trick-or-treating adventure ever!

#14: Miss Holly Is Too Jolly!
Mistletoe means kissletoe, the worst tradition in the history of the world!

#15: Mr. Macky Is Wacky!
Mr. Macky expects A.J. and his friends to read stuff about the presidents...and even dress up like them! He's taking Presidents' Day way too far!

#16: Ms. Coco Is Loco!
It's Poetry Month and the whole school is poetry crazy, thanks to Ms. Coco. She talks in rhyme! She thinks boys should have feelings! Is she crazy?

#17: Miss Suki Is Kooky!
Miss Suki is a very famous author who writes about endangered animals. But when her pet raptor gets loose during a school visit, it's the kids who are endangered!

#18: Mrs. Yonkers Is Bonkers!
Mrs. Yonkers builds a robot substitute teacher to take her place for a day!

#19: Dr. Carbles Is Losing His Marbles!
Dr. Carbles, the president of the board of education, is fed up with Mr. Klutz and wants to fire him. Will A.J. and his friends be able to save their principal's job?

#20: Mr. Louie Is Screwy!
When the hippie crossing guard, Mr. Louie, puts a love potion in the water fountain, everyone at Ella Mentry School falls in love!

#21: Ms. Krup Cracks Me Up!
A.J. thinks that nothing can possibly be as boring as a sleepover in the natural history museum. But anything can happen when Ms. Krup is in charge.